Eternal Love

Flairs and Glairs

Publication House

"Eternal Love"

ISBN No: " 978-93-90799-07-7"
1st Edition
Language – English and Hindi

Flairs and Glairs
Publication House
Regd. Under MSME Act.

Copyright. 2021, Vaishni Venkatesh

Disclaimer

This is a work of fiction and solely represent the thoughts of the corresponding authors of the articles. Our editors have tried their best to edit the content of all the authors and check the plagiarism.
All the write-ups in this book are unique and are only published in this book.
In case any plagiarism or error is found, only the author is responsible alone, and not the publisher or the Compilers.

Cover Designing and Book Formatting
Shubham Shah and Ishani Agarwal

About the Book

The anthology ETERNAL LOVE is an assortment of stories, open letter, and poetries expressing the never ending love of authors towards their parents, better half, friends, family members, profession, dream, goal, job, hobby, and their loved vocation.

Each author has penned down their endless love in such a way that you will feel enamoured, charmed, upbeat, and experience the heaven of love in the form of words. These authors have utilized their composition as divination to charm their perspective into your subconscious mind.

The main reason behind the publication of this anthology is to share the interminable love towards various things in life that continue moving dependent on the circumstance looked in every individual's life and to give a stage to authors to display their viewpoint in detail and get connected with the readers.

Acknowledgement

The formation of this treasury would not have been possible without the co-authors. Their experiences made this treasury an enchanted one. Much obliged to you co-authors, without your help and knowledge this compilation wouldn't be magical.

Thanks to everyone who has tried sincerely and has put forth attempts for this anthology to be a success.

I want to express my gratitude toward Anshu Malika Roja Selvamani for bringing me into this writing world. Without your persistent direction, I wouldn't have had the option to investigate and build up an enthusiasm for writing.

Above all, hearty thanks to my family and friends for supporting us throughout this anthology. I am thankful to Flairs and Glairs Publication without whom this project wouldn't have been possible.

I also thank Zeel Milishia for her constant guidance and support throughout this project

Lastly, I thank the almighty for giving me this opportunity and solidarity to complete this anthology successfully.

Co-Authors

Shubham Shah (Founder Flairs and Glairs)
Ishani Agarwal (Co-Founder Flairs and Glairs)

1. Vaishni Venkatesh (Compiler)
2. Anshu Malika Roja Selvamani
3. Moneshasree J
4. Rahul Yadav K
5. Rabhina Roy A P
6. Harshini Jayachandran
7. Oviyapriya K
8. Swetha Pichaipillai
9. Namratha Atluri
10. Santhosh Pandian A
11. Sajin Jenifer A S

Shubham Shah

(Founder- Flairs and Glairs)

Shubham Shah, an entrepreneur at "Flairs & Glairs" a brand with dynamics in events organizing and cultural educational pan INDIA, is a 26yrs old guy who recently has entered the digital platform of imprinting emotions. He has initiated with

his own open mic platform to help budding poets and aspiring writers under his brand named as "Teekhe Zasbaaat"

He is a commerce graduate from the Bhagalpur City of Bihar. He states Writing has impersonated him since childhood and he has now been writing for over a decade!

Cooking, on the other hand, is his passion! He also mentions, trying out new things just tickles him!

When asked sir, Why SPICY EMOTIONS?

He smiled and added, "agar jasbaat teekhe na ho toh wo jasbaat kahan" Spices are all that blends! So do his words!

As a chef, he presents to you his dish! Hot and freshly served! Taste it! Feel it! Enjoy it! You can also find his writing in the Book "Teekhe Zasbaaat" and 50+ Co-authored anthologies. With his passion to explore opportunities across Platforms, he is working with keen devotion and We wish him all the very best for his future ventures.

He is Featured in the **International Magazine De-Mode** for his upcoming solo novel.

He is **Approved by Ne8x for its Lit Fest,** and is a **Golden Star Awards 2020 Winner.**

He is an **India Book of Records Holder** for his Anthology **Satrang,** and has the **Grandmaster** title by **Asia Book of Records**, for the same.

He has also been featured in **Prabhat Khabar**, **Dainik Jagran** and other renowned Newspaper for his achievements. He has also been awarded with **India Star Republic Award 2021.**

He has been a proud co-author to

India Book of Records (Title- Black)

World Book of Records (Title -15 Wonders of Poetries)

India Book of Records (Title - Aaina)

Vajra World Records Holder (Title - Gustakhi Maaf Hai)

High Range of Records Holder (Title - Gustakhi Maaf Hai)

Share your reviews on his

INSTAGRAM

@spicy_emotions
@shubham4shah
Or via email on
shubham2shah@gmail.com

To stay tuned to his work and opportunities follow his business Handles

INSTAGRAM   FACEBOOK   YOUTUBE

@flairsandglairs
@teekhezasbaaat

WEBSITE:

https://flairsandglairs.in/
https://flairsandglairs.com/

Ishani Agarwal

(Co-Founder- Flairs and Glairs)

Ishani Agarwal hails from the City of Joy, Kolkata.
She is the co-founder of her Community "Teekhe Zasbaaat" and Flairs and Glairs Publication.
Been a Compiler for 45+ Anthologies, she is in the process for more. Co-authored in 150+ Anthologies. She is a India Book

of Records Holder, a Vajra World Records Holder, a High Range of Records Holder and a Bravo Record holder.

Approved by Ne8x for its Lit Fest 2020, and Literary Icon 2020. Also a Golden Star Awards Winner 2020.

She has also been awarded with India Star Republic Award 2021.

She has been featured by the National Magazine "Taree Zameen Par" with the title 'unstoppable'.

Also featured in the International Magazine DeMode for her upcoming solo novel, she is proud to write on social issues, and is happy with the love she is receiving.

Connect with her on Instagram: @Ishani_agarwal_quotes / @compilations_so_far

VAISHNI VENKATESH
(COMPILER)

Vaishni Venkatesh is Senior Executive – Corporate Sales at Naukri a strong sub-brand of Info edge India. Born and brought up in Chennai. She is a witty marketer, Electronic and Instrumentation engineer by profession completed her BE & MBA (Marketing & HR) from Jeppiaar Engineering College & St. Joseph's College of Engineering. She has also completed her Diploma in Digital marketing. She is a motivational speaker who is ambitious and charismatic.

She has been a resource person and speaker for many events, seminars, open mics, and also the MC of several events. She has grown out to be reckoned with confidence and liveliness personified on stage.

She believes that kindness will conquer the world. She draws a solution for every problem beautifully on her wrist. She loves to write because she reach people through her writing. She enjoys sharing knowledge and guiding everyone towards their goals.

She contributes her active participation in volunteering and social service. She is a person who believes that ultimate purpose of life is not achieving only one's goal but to help the needy as much as possible.

She is an author, orator, compiler, epigrammatist, and artist. She is passionate about research, digital marketing, writing books, compiling anthologies & being co-author in anthologies as well. She is also experienced in event management and event organizing.

She aims to be an entrepreneur who can serve the nation by developing students' talents and guiding them in the right path. She has her own food blog with mouth-watering recipes, and reviews named LAFOODBINGE. She aims to change the society and be a trendsetter.

Instagram ID: vaishni_venkatesh

BEING A WRITER

It's been almost 5 days and I have not given my solo book even a solitary pinnacle. I figured I ought to have a break, I needed to quit running persistently on this so-called passion and career ground. Just to unlearn how life would be if I am not a writer, not workaholic, not an individual who takes a ton of stress and pressure and finishing all work on time, just denying all work allocated. Wait, that is really not a possible one. Yet, I checked it out. Soon my author's psyche began to long about what my solo book actually move.

Welcome you into the writers world!!!

Would it be advisable for me to make it a spine chiller or make my hero the superhuman or would it be advisable for me to go on with the real time incidents connected like those constellations. I spoke to strangers, I listened to their stories, started to spend time speaking with nature, and yes even with creatures to be honest. I was literally having a lot of fun. Now back to being a writer. So we have a lot of work to be done.

Now I woke up, fresh enough to start with my manuscript, with laptop all ready and rushing to the kitchen for some espresso. In any case, isn't it better to write in a bistro instead of composing on my own lawn? So off to the bistro I request my #1 latte and rush to get the seat close to the window. Much the same as how the seat close to the window in buses have its own fan base.

Okay so fast like the light flipped my laptop, opening previous draft, chapter 3, page number 4, line number eighteen what should my protagonist do? Pick way A or way B. Should I go with majority peoples mindset or my rare preference? Okay let me go back to have glimpses of what actually my character's true

shades are. Is there a problem with the premise. Not again! Am I stuck again with the same situation?

After a gap of 3 hrs, gulped 2 latte and 3 pastries. May be let me take a walk, meeting strangers, more chances of them resembling my protagonist. Yet, they appear to be completely known people after all it's the bistro close to my condo! One wave of wind which takes my thoughts away from my script.

NO! NO! focus.

So this idea of writing in bistro doesn't work. Back to home, becoming the night owl, buried in complete isolation. Silence prevailing all around me. You know night time is the perfect time to write. No aggravation No failure and finally I will have the option to focus on my content. Okay, so let's make the position comfortable. Moving from bed to consider the table and afterward to the couch and last to the love seat close to the window, History rehashes! Love for windows never blur. So pull off the curtains.

Back to writing from the situation I paused my protagonist to take a proper decision. So with my headsets on with changing the music from melody to folk to customary Carnatic music, I know Carnatic music is actually the most noticeably terrible thought yet that is how it took all my time to settle down with a soothing song. So all day I sit and finally I brought some spin in this skit. So now comes the U-turn in the story and getting deeper into the characters vibe.

So exactly after 1 week of rest and seeking of a comfortable place with tuning the wavering mind back into the perfect phase, the work is accomplished. Wait so there emerges my uncertainty, why is my protagonist story moving on a melancholy boat? Is it a miserable story? No yaar, life isn't generally hopeless. I think my protagonist is in deficiency of conviction. But I just gave an

ambition prescription. Would it be a good idea for me to change the plotline, is it being excessively odd? Sooner or later, everything I could compose was a speck, dab, and dab in light of the fact that my cerebrum has just got disappointed to envision what will be the decision of my protagonist. Is this the ideal one? Heaps of inquiries slamming my head without a stop. No, I am not suffering temporarily from the writer's block!!!

And my child is suffering from severe chronic content disorder. So now I am completely hopeless, how am I going to complete this book, I am speechless. So here tells the writer in me "Attempt till u receive the best in return" no more demotivating. Stimulated back with my pen stacking it with the ink of feelings and shooting expressions of the correct choice. So as I murmur the lines my fingers began to tap on the correct keys with the correct speed and time. Relentless writing, though being a night owl my stomach begins to give those peculiar snarls. I need to feed myself in order to feed my protagonist with future innovations.

So here comes a series of draft, draft on loop. Once I have started I will never stop untill I reach the destiny. So I kept on writing. So I can feel as what kind of person I have evolved. So I kept on writing without any clog. Unveiling the mystery behind the lessons of life. After the perpetual fight with a lot of words and still I am the writer so it is always possible for me to change the story from sad to a happily ever after. At last it is not easy being a writer. But I choose this as my vocation. Because my passion towards writing was secondary and my love towards writing is always endless.

My eternal love was always for writing, because I found it the expression of my thoughts recorded in books with the company of millions of words…

HOW I FEEL WHILE WRITING

Have you ever discovered sitting on sands close to the seashore? Have you tasted the outside air with the mitigating sound of the waves gradually contacting your internal soul? The scent of sand and the flavor of the air makes your heart sink in the ocean of harmony. That is how I feel when I write. Like I am doing a deep meditation before my laptop screen. Like I am gathering the shells from the beach and gluing with my words on paper promptly. As I experience all these, there begins the craving for writing to express how I feel. The way these words make me feel. The manner in which they change from obscure dialects to profound sentiments and feelings. So they change totally into living creatures hopping close to me. Butterflies all over me, that is how I feel.

Like the canines pursuing vehicles, thoughts and perspectives begin pursuing my cerebrum. With my fingers caught in plants pushing me to compose what I feel. Like the butterflies glinting their wings, recollections continue blazing with excellent shades of tones. How valuable are these words? They interface my heart to everything. They make me buzzing with letters. It is the way I talk with you and it is the manner in which I feel the musicality and tune all over me. We are portraying the story having a mug of latte and inclining close to the window. How insane feel it is. How violently phenomenal it is, that I am gifting my words to you straightforwardly into your hands. Furthermore, treat you with those confections between your tongue and teeth.

To be enamoured with the page that might communicate your musings. To be enamoured with the pen who might

communicate your feeling. Being a writer is like to be in love, An Eternal Love

That is how I feel when I write. It is not only about writing, it completes the whole saga of expressing myself and what I think. It finishes the entire adventure of communicating my opinion. This ceaseless adventure of affection for composing, narrating, making sonnets, spurring, depicting the excellence of every single species on this planet.

Indeed, it is a blessing what writer are blessed with. I choose to be a writer and I am proud of my decision.

This world can change, but my love towards being a writer will never change. And that's how my eternal love remains everlasting.

DEAR WRITER IN ME,

Where do I start about the thing my heart is stating? This distance between us has removed me from my circuit. All your memories makes me eager throughout the evening. My heart isn't tuning in to me to quit contemplating you. You are a sweet intoxication in my life that can never be taken out. In your contemplations, my life seems to be available in blurred vision.

It had a place with me yet now it is behaving like an outsider. Once in a while I chime in and think back your recollections. I sing the song of praising you. You ought to acknowledge how crazy I am about you. I am as yet uncertain about whether you are a figment or genuine. At the point when my heart sees you, it runs behind you like a pup who loves to see its proprietor.

We should simply break this glass among us and meet soon. The facts confirm that you have enslaved me. Has anyone extended a treacherous spell on me? I am charmed by you. You burn my cheek with your name. Making a deep scar may be a scar of love? We were like birds flying in the opposite direction but now we have become partners.

Meeting you resembled somebody dear to me. It resembled we had some connection for many lives. The stars sparkled brilliantly when I saw you unexpectedly and the fireflies began to focus their light alongside the blue spark between us, it all accounts like a fantasy, in any case, Isn't this an indication of genuine romance or endless love? ETERNAL LOVE? The concentration on you makes me not to be in spotlight on the

race of my life. Brimming with interruption about you make me crave for you more than my studies.

Indeed, I am in distraught love with you my dear writing. You have recently come into my life in a flash however now turned into my lifeline. More love towards you urges me to compose more and to communicate my inclination and emotions as words. And you have just changed my whole life more expressive, more enjoying, more self-obsessed, and more addictive.

You assist me with spreading my point of view and impression of the world and moreover permitted me to talk boisterously for the right condition. So in some cases because of circumstances, we may be isolated however we should be together perpetually till my last breathe in so I can discover more about myself. You are the examiner who opens my perception and my internal soul to new things. Will continue writing because it has become difficult now to live without you.

Your passionate writer,
Vaishni Venkatesh

ANSHU MALIKA ROJA SELVAMANI

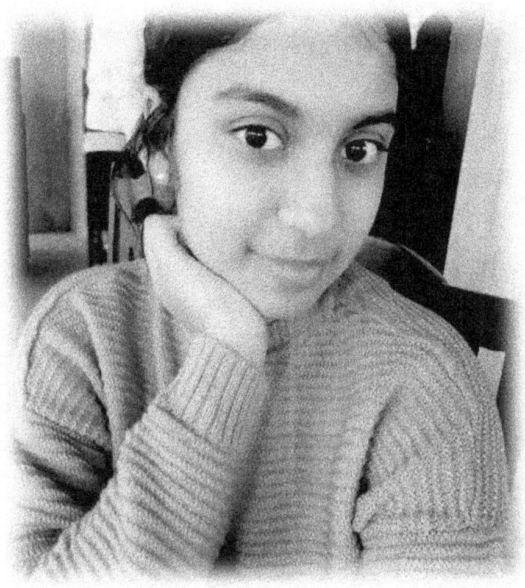

Anshu Malika Roja Selvamani was brought up in Hyderabad. She is just in high school but is already writing books.

She's a very expressive, shy and creative young girl. She believes she can change the world with her writing. She has faced different circumstances in her life which she strongly thinks has shaped her ideas and work. She is an award winning writer who has won the innovative writer award from Vivekanada Youth Parliament.

She loves adventure and travelling, most importantly she loves to weave her experiences and fantasies into touching stories.

Email ID: anshucandy345@gmail.com

THE LOVE WAR

It felt like love was around,
So I turned to see it blow,
In deep desires to feel it flow,
Nude cheeks turned pink,
I felt it sink,
That I was indeed in love,
His silhouette began to make appearances,
I felt the world disappear into light,
His silhouette still stood bright,
The icy white mountains shrunk in front of my love,
The deep blue oceans vanished,
Sitting in my room I was conquered,
Conquered by love,
Conquered by reminiscence,
Conquered by his faint appearance still visible,
How he looked like I had never a clue,
Around a summer I saw him out of the blue,
The winds hit against my bony cheeks,
The skin froze,
The blood was still warm,
Love was my warmth,
Imagining his hands around my shoulders,
Thinking about him all night,
Forced to fight sleep,
Searching for him every day,
I spent time in every place in our town,
In deep desires to find him and not his silhouette,
It was fear,
Fear that his silhouette would never turn real,
If that was the truth,
One day my heart would tear,
I wish it would be just a fear,
Love was around,

It held me tight all angles it surrounded,
Love was a feeling so new,
It chose to surround only a few,
Astonishing it was to see people find love in the most
unexpected of times,
Some with a person,
Some with money,
Some with food,
Some with fame,
To me love was a different mood,
A mood that kept me awake at nights,
A mood that left me feeling warm,
People whisper around me always,
So used to hearing "she doesn't even know how he looks
like" I was,
Love doesn't come from looks,
Love comes from no defined place,
Different for everyone it comes in different forms,
I was in love not with his face,
A heart he had that was golden,
I caught him helping wounded children,
A golden heart is worth more than treasures man can ever
discover,
A golden heart was what I fell in love with

MONESHASREE J

Moneshasree is from Chennai, currently doing her third year in MBA integrated at St. Josephs college of engineering. She is good at her studies. She is a kind of girl who puts her maximum effort in everything she does. She is excellent in pencil sketching and also a wonderful nature admirer. She is a girl who always makes others feel comfortable. She is a good classical dancer and also a girl who strives hard to taste success.

MAMAN JE T'AIME

The word eternal means no beginning, no ending always continuing. Eternal love is the love that is so strong external force, and is endless.

Such love is always a better feeling for each and everyone in this universe. From my side I would say "mom's love" as eternal love. Let me start sharing my opinion on Mom's love.

Mah, the love you have for me is always eternal (ie). endless. The child who lose their mother longs for her love and the one who is blessed always tries to ignore it.

You were the only soul who satisfied my hunger by giving your blood in the form of breast milk, "the soul with no added preservatives".

We all know the proverb " We never know the value of water until the well goes dry", the same way I never knew the value of your love which I received from you were with me. We never value anything which is received so easily.

You are the trustworthy soul with whom I can share my feelings, emotions this and that etc... I never forget to say each and everything whatever happens from the time I wake up and till I go to bed. This gives a big satisfaction as if I have done something great.

You are always possessive and selfish towards. You always want me to be the best, to get everything, and never care about others. You always see whether I am blessed with everything.

The love for something which is invisible is always precious. Imagination towards something is always a sweet feeling. You started loving me from the day you started carrying me in you.

You don't even know how I look, how I care for you, how I behave towards you, you knew nothing about me, but still you loved me truly without any expectations. I hope you felt blessed when your imagination became true.

And mah, I always feel that my Maths teacher is far better compared to you, so strict but still you feel for me truly and those are eternal and endless things I get from you wherever I am and whatever I do.

You thought we how to speak, thought me what is right and which is wrong. You carried me 10 months in your womb and rest of the life in your heart. Wherever you're, your blessings will never forget to reach me.

Mommy I even want to say about the way you provide me food, with love and care etc... Paah! What a cooking missing those delicious food mom.

Especially I love your feeding, I still wonder what a magical hands you have, the food which you feed me with your magical hands are soooooooooooo yummy and tasty. Need these feelings till my last breath mommy.

Mom you are really a priceless creature, which can't be bought with n number of money. I can appoint a guardian to do all the work and take care of me, I can even call her mother but none in this world can replace you in my heart my love, your care your emotions towards me, I consider it to be priceless and a blessing.

You always motivate me and keep me fully charged you never let my battery level go low. If I am this much today it's fully because of your motivation and trust you had on me.

You're motivation and love is the secret of my energy. A tight hug and cute little kiss in my cheeks is the best painkiller I ever realized. However big the problem maybe just a 2 minutes talk with you is enough for me to feel refreshed and think what to do next.

Love to have such a mother like you so supportive and encouraging, always want to make my dreams come true, so understanding. I always wonder so this is called as love. Always making me feel comfortable. Whatever problems you face you never try to show it to me, such a smiling face.

Your love is my drug and I am so much addicted, nothing else is so proud than saying I am your daughter. I hurt you, irritate you, disturb you and do all mischievous things but still there is no change in you, You still love me the same, do all good to me, these make me feel and understand how true your love is.

There is no substitute for you mommy. Just saying I love you is never enough for all those you did and waiting do for me, but still I knew you expect the same true love from my side, which I always have for you.
I just want to spend rest of my life holding your hands tighter and enjoying each and every minute with you my dear...
MOM'S LOVE IS ALWAYS ENDLESS AND ETERNAL...
Love you my mother...

RAHUL YADAV K

The most practical and realistic person you can ever meet and a fun-loving person. A brilliant writer in the genre Love and Romance. A name synonymous with "Relationship" and a character filled with discipline and dignity and always lives up to the line "Format Past and Restart Love". He is vocal and practices the essence of being Multidimensional. Fun is in his DNA and his sense of humour is its testimony. Knowing him up close creates unwavering craziness.

I.C.U

When your time is limited you have to spend it to be happy. Sadly, she can't do that. It's been more than a year since she was confined to the ICU. Months of suffering and loneliness. Accidents are a part of life; some are good and some are bad. But have you ever come across such accident which can change YOU?

Your whole life? The way you think? Your emotions? Well, the same happened with this girl. A person who loves to travel, loves to explore.

I first met her in my college. She's there for a Youth Festival. It's the night time. The moons delicate light had just turned the world a-flame with silver when I saw her. She had an attractive figure. Her curvilinear waist didn't surprise me as much as the saffron tint to her complexion. She must be a native, I thought to myself. Her crescent shaped eyebrows inclined slightly as she saw me staring at her. I yelped at being caught.

And then it happened. Her delicate eyelashes of velvet-black blinked once slowly, as if to invite me to her. When I came closer, I happened to notice her ears, nose, eyes very near to me. It was not just LOVE AT FIRST SIGHT. It was LOVE AT FIRST LIGHT.

Her luminous, heavenly-white teeth flashed as she smiled looking at me. Her hair was a glorious tumble of star beam-gold and her virility-brown eyes set my heart a-thump. Her lips. Her red lips. Her god damn red lips. There was no word left to express that beauty. Her elegant personality, all mesmerized me. It was never that easy to describe. I couldn't talk to her. She left the place after a while. I really felt sad for not being able to talk to her.

Sometimes in life's worst moments, we realize how strong and resilient we truly are. And in those moments – our vulnerability can allow magic to happen.

It was just after 10pm on that day – a beautiful night in Bangalore. I was driving home from the youth festival in college, from Indira

Nagar to HSR Layout– the same stretch of road I had been driving for two years now.

It had rained the day before, but this particular night was clear, so I didn't think anything of it as I drove the normal speed limit. Suddenly, my steering wheel felt funny and started to shake. The road looked shiny.

Before I could blink, I was straddling the two highway lanes, surrounded by two barriers, no shoulder in sight. I had no control. A rush of terror and fear came over me as I helplessly slid across the road. I started screaming for my life.

My passenger door hit the cement rail to the right. Like a bumper car, I started spinning. And then, I hit a barrier head on and was now perpendicular to oncoming traffic. I tried turning my wheel. No luck in favour of me.

I turned to look out my passenger window. Lights were coming towards me. I couldn't stop it. All I could do was scream – please no, please no! This wasn't my time. But the headlights kept getting closer and before I knew it --

BOOM.

My car started spinning.

BOOM. Hit again.

Finally, I stopped spinning and found myself facing a wall of oncoming headlights. The smell of smoke filled my car and I panicked, thinking my car was on fire. But I couldn't get out. Both of my doors were smashed in and stuck. My fear overwhelmed me further.

Suddenly, my door opened

"Are you ok? Are you hurt? I'm a firefighter." He spoke.

I jumped out of my car and collapsed on the floor of the highway. The rush of fear and emotion was too much. As the firefighter tried to calm me down, I turned and looked at all the headlights in the distance. They were so close. So close to a much different ending. Instead, there were only two cars involved in the accident. One was mine. Who's was the other? (I thought).

There we were, two cars, one black, one white, perfectly parked next to each other, both facing the wrong way, staring at endless miles of headlights.

Soon the police were there. They ceased the place and started to enquire. After a while, one policeman told me I should feel sorry for the driver of the other car.

"Feel sorry for the driver who hit me? Why? Holy shit. Even I was a victim of the incident" I thought. Then he proceeded to tell me that if it weren't for the other driver, I wouldn't be lying on a bed in the nearby hospital right now.

I was really shocked to hear that.

Who was it? What happened to him? How is that guy? Is he Okay? I asked the policemen.

He just said one answer. "It's a girl who was on the driving seat and now she's admitted in the nearby Hospital. Her condition is critical as of now."

A sense of sympathy flowed out of my heart for her. I was trying to help myself move to the hospital walking on the highway leaving my broken car aside.

I rushed into the emergency ward with the blood flowing out of the torn parts of my dress.

"Doctor!" (I shouted). "Who is it?" I asked (very impatient).

The stranger, who I later learned was that girl (yes, my Angel), pulled her emergency break and was able to gain control of her car. Instead of t-boning me, she side-swiped me, and quickly hit the hazards to notify the other cars behind him.

But she couldn't realise the thing happened to her. She was bleeding all around. She couldn't notice herself with the intention of turning the accident off. GOD!!

"How is she Doctor?" I asked (breathing abnormally).

"Her body is severely damaged and her brain had a concussion. Can never say when she's going to recover." Doctor said.

I tried to enquire who she is. No one from my college knows who she is. *"Why the fuck did she appear at the Youth Festival."* *"Why the fuck didn't I talk to her before she left the place"*

Hers is a newly registered car. I couldn't find her address. *"How the fuck in the world can I know her details." "God! Give me a way."*

Not one missing case is registered for the next one week. *"Who is this girl?"*

My family soon arrived to the hospital and advised me to go to my hometown.

"Dad, I wrecked her car and she saved my life. I should be here till she recovers – it was the least I could do." I spoke.

After thirty minutes of debate with them, they left and I was staying at my friends' place near the hospital praying for her recovery. I was used to going to hospital early in the morning and returning late night. I just had one question in my mind. "WHO IS SHE?"

Time is running out so fast. And life is starting to slip away but I didn't give up. I kept on hoping for a miracle to happen. One year passed since the accident on the highway and she is still confined in the hospital. She might not be wishing to live like this.

I was sitting on the bench outside I.C.U when a little girl approached me. The little girl was really cute. Brown eyes and chubby cheeks. I bet this girl will break thousands of hearts in the future. I thought.

"Can you help me find Room No. 310?" the little girl asked me.

"Sure." Then I pinched the little girl's cheeks.

"I think this is room 310. May I ask who is here?" I asked the girl.

"Come inside and I'll introduce you to him." The girl held my hands and led me inside. The state of the man inside shocked me. Tubes and wires were all over his body. Then the girl sat beside the guy.

"You know what, this guy is really good. He would always look out for others. He always had a smile on his face though he was really lonely. Behind the happy-go-lucky attitude was a guy hoping to be loved. Too bad he's still sleeping for a year already."

"A year?" I thought.

I looked at how the little girl cares for her brother. What a lovely and sad sight it was. I used to go every day to the same room. Spend some time with that little girl and the patient. Day by day, I got more closer to the siblings. The love they share. It attracts me the most. One day, few school girls visited her when they are on break. After they went back to their school, I asked the little one.

"Why you're not going to school?"

"I am not willing to leave my brother unless and until he's completely recovered."

"Nurses and Doctors are there for him, right?"

"But there is no LOVE from me." She said.

"So, you are coming to help him and be with him."

"Not exactly. I am here giving respect to the Love my brother shared with me all these years." She said.

"Who is ready to give his/her complete life to a patient who is in coma for more than one year unless he/she is loving them." She continued.

With a blank face I returned to the room in which my girl is admitted. I saw her face with the oxygen mask put from the transparent door.

Is this LOVE? I thought. It's been more than one year. I don't know. I'll be waiting for her to open her eyes once.

And one night, the miracle happened. Nurses and Doctors are panicking everywhere. There is a disturbance in the hospital. She is out of the coma. I am glad to see her active after one and a half year.

After thirty minutes, she became conscious. I went to see her and thank her and if possible, talk to her.

"Hi. I am Arjun." I said. "How are you feeling now? Is everything good?"

I am shocked to hear what she said.

"I LOVE YOU. I cannot risk my life again without saying this to you. That day, I was heading back to your college to propose you, but then the accident happened. Even till the last second, I was hoping to be safe to come and talk to you. But it all happened. I

am so happy that it's you with me after these many months. I LOVE YOU ARJUN. My parents died 2 years back and I have no one left for me. Will you accept my love?" She said

"Shocked of course. Who will expect this? But my answer is expected."

"I Love you too. I Love you more. I Loved You from the moment I saw you."

"I just have one question. Can I ask?" I said.

"What?"

"Your Name?"

"Priyanka"

"I Love You Priyanka." I said.

Thanks to the little girl for reminding me about my love towards Priyanka. Even after Priyanka is discharged, we used to go to Room No. 310 and spend an hour with them every day.

It's NEVER THE END----

A P RABHINA ROY

Through this piece of text our author A.P.Rabhina Roy despite her young age has taken her time to write this marvellous text. Like the saying "Roses donot bloom hurriedly" ,our writer has taken her time to give us this masterpiece.

Instagram ID: __.rabhii.__

A FOODIE'S LOVE

Endless love means loving without any restrictions ,continuing that for eternity Everything in the world has a limit except love. In my life there is no end for my love. It may be a person or things, my love has no end. I love each and every favorite. There are many thing , I love but now I want you share about 4 things

Food

Best friend (Friends are my first love)

Pets and animals

Self-love

When I talk about food ,this quote by John Walters comes to my mind, "The only thing I like better than talking about food is eating "

My favourite thing in the world is food !The reason behind this is ,our life is for enjoyment, how much eve we earn ,we have to eat daily We need it daily just to keep our life going. I prefer non veg over veg and I eat both without any restraints ,the young age is the only time we can do that! Words can't express my appreciation and love for food .I always keep in mind that I shouldn't waste food .

Foods are of different forms all around the world ,there is Italian ,Chinese etc ...

But tandoori is my all-time favourite. A peaceful day with tandoori chicken would make me the happiest person in the entire world. My life should be for earning and helping people, for that i need strength for that ,food Is important for that .We can't always depend on others to get us food ,so I started cooking !i forget to mention sweets !while my parents make

delicious sweets in the kitchen,I just wait for them to finish so that I can devour them !

However there is a catch !if we take in anything more than necessary for our body it isn't good for our health ,most people in India suffer from diabetes and are over weight !! So consume everything moderately!

When I was young Child ,I used to waste a lot of food

But now I don't ,because I realise how there are so many people don't get what's normal for us .Please my readers stop wasting food and enjoy life to the fullest.

EXTREME ENDEARMENT!

Friendship -Another important and favourite part of my life is friendship .We meet so many people in life ,some are just passing clouds where as some stay with us forever! Those ones make our life better and try to help us with everything they can .Everyone has their good qualities as well as bad ,our parents try and see only the good in us ,However as we open up to our friends more ,they know more about us and they know our bad qualities too.i think the best relationship that makes life worth living is friendship !Every relationship has their ups and downs ,that makes the friendship stronger !

For a good relationship both sides should learn to be adjusting.Making friends in school ,at a age where the biggest problem is forgetting a pencil case at home is so pure and precious.If those friends come along with us the entire life ,they would witness our goals as well as achievements in life .School life becomes more enjoyable due to friends ,just aimlessly wandering and having fun,u woudnt get anything like that in your life ever again !Every friend wants him /her and myself to reach the greatest heights in life ,

The quote ,"Teamwork makes dream work " resonated with me when I found how one true friend can get you past the strongest of storms without asking anything in return.I guess that's why I prioritise friends so much !

Not everyone can find someone they completely be themselves,I have such few nice people in my life .I am forever grateful and appreciate them for hanging around with me.

Like me if you have few such friends ,trust me and don't ever let them go!

LOVE FOR MY ANIMAL FRIENDS!

My love for pets and generally just animals!

I'm ready to everything I can to give a better world for animals .How much ever stressed we are our pets have the ability to reduce our stress to nothing in just few minutes. All of us have gone to the zoo at least once in our life ,we would see animals all caged up and it would give me such sadness and would we want that to happen to us ??Animals are imprisoned without doing any crime !Would we be normal if that happened to us ?We destroyed their home ground and built buildings and captured them for our liking .

In the forest areas ,there might be scarcity for water because we take all the resources in the entire world for us !We are just being selfish !!!

Wild animals cannot be tamed ,so even if we wanted to help them ,there are high chances that they might attack us .But pet animals are controllable and they do understand us to some extent!

Why pets are found adorable?

They give us something humans fail to give ourselves, the unconditional love we receive without any judgement, that makes us feel like the best person !Waking and finding your pet waiting for you ,or entering your house after a long work day and seeing your pet wagging its tail at you is the best feeling ever!!!

Now ,can you get any living thing to love you unconditionally without any judgement?

The answer is no !

Then we should treat them the best !

Let's make the world better for them ,let's not take them granted and make the world suitable for them.

IS SELF LOVE SELFISHNESS?

"If you are searching for that one person that will change your life ,take a look in the mirror " This is one of the quotes that initiated me to get me out of my comfort zone.

Everyone has their affection and love for their parents, friends ,other close relations etc ..but when it comes to them ,they fail there.

But not me ,I love myself !I appreciate every part of me. My legs for taking me places ,my hands that makes me do miraculous work ,my heart that keeps me going !When you truly love yourself for the person that you are ,you become invincible ,you can't let others stop you at any cost ,You are the boss of your life !

Let's say that I'm facing a problem ,only I can get myself out of that ,no one will lend their hand ! If you want to stay depressed or sad ,then you will stay that way ,in the snap of your finger if you decide you want to change things around and stay happy only you can do it .

Others always judge and compare self-love to selfishness! Every one cannot always live for others all the time ,they have to make decision for their well-being after all it is their life! No one can love us more than we do ourselves. When you start to believe in yourselves you can bend a bridge .Even the biggest obstacle will seem like a small grain, the impossible will seem possible.

There will be times where we would feel lonely ,but if you love yourself and know how to take care of yourself those feelings won't be there ,you will know how to keep yourself occupied.

Self-love is not given that much importance so please start practising it .Start everyday by saying 5 good things about yourself ,put on a face mask, treat yourself, watch a movie that you love! Prioritise yourself ,develop your own opinion and love yourself and live your best life!

HARSHINI JAYACHANDRAN

Harshini Jayachandran, an aspiring engineer pursuing Electronics and Instrumentation engineering, is an amateur writer who has just started attempting writing anthologies. Her epigram towards writing is an iterate by Benjamin Franklin, "Either write something worth reading, or do something worth writing".

Instagram ID: _.harshini._ _

AMOUR PROPRE!

Prioritizing yourself, take yourself on a date, make your body happy, express yourself, write a love letter to yourself; these are the ventures we attempt on account of self-love. Self-love simply communicates having a high consideration and concern for your own well-being and happiness.

"Treat yourself with a boost of self-love everyday it'll help you spread your wings wide enough and fly high with a peak level of energy''. Before expecting somebody else to love us, We ourselves must start implementing our love for ourselves. Deciphering what self-love looks like for you as an individual is a predominant part of each individual's mental health. If you're a person whose just gonna start implementing self-love in your daily life all you have to do is: Talk to yourself with love, give yourself a complete break from self-judgment, trust yourself and keep going with a good level of self-confidence, even if you find practising this strenuous initially, Am damn sure this is gonna give you colossal glee at a point.

Self-love actually means tackling yourself as you are at this moment and feel rapturous for everything that you are. So My dear readers my sycophantic appeal to you all is, at this very moment accept yourself completely just the way you are. Self-love always stimulates you to make flourishing options in life. When you clasp yourself on high esteem, you're more likely to choose things that bring up your well-being and aid you well. Practice good self-care, when you take better care of your basic needs you will love yourself more eventually. Start practising self-love by being kind, patient and gentle to

yourself, just the way you would to someone who means everything to you.

"Your greatest responsibility is to love yourself and to know you are enough". Let all of us start being our own reason to smile always!

SOLICITUDE FOR MY PASSION-WRITING!

I've always wanted keep myself occupied with some pursuit that would make my entity beneficial at some point, but never got a chance to do it or I would keep on shilly-shallying and persuading myself that it isn't important now and it can wait…it can wait like my whole survival can be manifested on thinking about it. That is when writing anthologies was scattered into my intellect by a soul, whom I appraise to be one of the very few predominant people in my life. The soul I broached above is none other than, the very much chivalrous Ms. Vaishni Venkatesh. She is more than a sister from another mother kinda substance to me. The love, endearment and reverence I have towards her is, and always will endure to be eternal and endless forever. She is my mentor, my confidante, my angel, my endorser and so on…Words would never be ample to asserrate my hat tip to her. My dear respectful sister Ms. Vaishni Venkatesh, thanks for sowing into me the magnificent kernel of knowledge towards writing; The adoration and devotion I have towards you will always abide to be one and the same persistently and you will always remain as one of the predominant people in my life till it terminates forever.

Now coming to my writing which I consider to be the most esteemed zeal of mine. Writing has always been an exceptional chill out to me. Whenever I agonize from extraneous stumbling blocks such as mental trauma, despair due to collapse etc; writing was my only lifesaver. I would always pen down my convictions as it will lead to the dearth

of my mental stress. Writing will always endure to be the most predominant zeal of mine.

My epigram towards writing is an iterate by Benjamin franklin ,"Either write something worth reading, or do something worth writing", But my dear zeal, I assure you that never in my life I'll terminate writing even if I do something worth reading!

ARDOUR FOR MY AMIGOS!

Throughout the last few years. I've comprehended so much above everlasting loyal love, and all that I realized was the significance of pursuing relationships and adjoining yourself with people who get you on a soul extent.

Obiviously all of us have people who enter and exit our lives – seasonal friends, But at this very moment I am very much thankful for those few, genuine friends in my life who I never have to interrogate. They show up in each and every walks of my life.

Friendship upto me is one kind of very special, genuine, loyal love and endearment that only a few succeed lifelong. It is someone trusting in the best in you forever; It's someone fortifying you at times when even you fail to fortify yourself; It's someone who keeps on pushing you to be the best version of yourself and is the first to applaud whenever you succeed. "A Friend is one who overlooks your broken fence and admires the flowers in your garden".

The most amazing hugs, the resounding laughter, The threatening walk away and yet stay back without any need of giving up on each other; The funniest hangouts, the nicknames being called, the sharing of secrets and such a lot more without any serious and weighty expectations or demands, I believe friendship is truly the best relationship one could make in this world.

Edith Wharton once said "I Suppose there is one friend in the life of each of us who seems not a separate person, however dear and beloved, but an expansion, an interpretation of one's self, the very meaning of one's soul", and this up to me is one

great illustration of true and loyal friendship. Always put your friends before yourself and rejoice over the things that make them happy; Build great faith and trust on one another, Provide your friends with a comfortable space that will always enable them to confide in you , all of these will enable your friendship to last longer with enormous amount of unconditional love.

Friendship is the only bond that lasts longer than any other bond because of one strong element in it which even a love-relationship fails, and that is "no exceptions or demands". Ralph Waldo Emerson once quoted, "The glory of friendship is not the outstretched hand, not the kindly smile, nor the joy of companionship, it is the spiritual inspiration that comes to one when you discover that someone else believes in you and is willing to trust you with a friendship";

To the few loyal pals I've got till date, Thanks for being there for me whenever I felt top of the world and also whenever I needed a shoulder to cry and I Love you all so much from the bottom of my heart !

TO SUM UP WITH MY ENDLESS LOVE!

Unconditional love is an hefty term for something that most of us don't really apprehend. The locution unconditional love or eternal love does not mean love without limits or bounds, It means "I offer you my love freely without any conditions applied"; which simply means that when we offer our love, we offer it without any expectations or demands in return.

Loving someone in hardships, mistakes and frustrations is a simple way of unconditional love. Compassionate love or a Agape love might sound somewhat familiar which simply means, you love freely and expect or demand nothing in return except their happiness.

The love you shower upon the almighty and indeed the abundant blessings you are blessed with is a sign of unconditional or eternal love from the creator; The love your parents treat you with, that awesome love in friendship, the genuine and loyal love between the life partners, all these are supremely unconditional.

"Spend your time on those that love you unconditionally. Don't waste it on those that only love you when the condition is right for them". When we spread love into the world, we share our gifts, time and talents with those around us. We genuinely want them to be happy and keep smiling always.

So my dear readers, I've spoken about three unconditional love domains I consider predominant, they are
Self-love
Love for pals
Love for passion

Hope you read and had a close endearment with my context, "Unconditional love is knowing someone's weakness and not taking an advantage of them. Knowing their flaws and accepting who they are, just the way they are". So let's all spread love to the extreme extent till our lives terminate forever.

OVIYAPRIYA K

Oviyapriya is a 23 years old girl who is doing her MBA. She is living in chengalpattu. She is a common girl who especially loves to be soft and easy in her life. So she finds her way accordingly. She loves to surrender her thoughts and suggestions so that one may benefit. She strives for a happy heart and healthy environment. By the way she wants her readers also to be benefitted. Thats why she pen down this piece of information.

Instagram ID: fan_of_dora

LET THE SEASON OF LOVE BEGINS!

Hey Charms.....!! Yeah, it's you. I exactly can't predict which would delight you. But I can reveal a secret about you. Guess what?

Charms.., come on...!! Try out know....!!

Okay relax! Let me tell you. Show me your ears. You are having an endless love on something. It may be a person, a place, a thing or it may be anything, but it means you a lot. It makes you to feel special in the Universe like nobody else can do. It may bless you with million dollar smile. See you are thinking about that one special material and delighting now! Is it? This feeling is cute know? I can hunch it from your heart. What is this endless mean?

Is it a numeric value? Or Scientific value?

If your answer is Yes, then my answer would be No. Even infinity has to end somewhere, but someone's feeling on other doesn't have a limit till their soul gets vanished. But fortunately one's soul will not fade because the soul lives until the universe fully diminishes. This is the real implication of endless.

This is the most special thing in the world that we all have limitless feeling on something which may or may not be related to us and especially without any expectations over that. Surplus of those feelings is universally referred as Love. Do I make sense?

Loving something is a super power that everybody is blessed with.

Super power?

Charms...! By the way, please don't wave your hands for a magical pen or that kind of stuffs. Of course that super power can do the greatest magic without a magic stick. What's that? Can you get me? No?

Okay. Continue surfing. You may get me now!

Loving something has a magical power of ignoring negativity from each cell your body. No no. Am not crazy! Okay, try out an experiment to get me. Think of a stuff on which you have a limitless love when you are feeling down or bad. Surely, that would change your mood of negativity. That feeling takes you to the world of comfort, joy and delight. By that time your depression would fly off. You start to recollect the past or move into the future with your love.

You know what? I have limitless love on lots and lots of stuffs. Let me share it so that I want my charms to accurately find on what you have an endless love, if you think that you are not a person who actually wants to keep your love on something.

I have n number of things to love because love is precious which is affordable!

Well dressed! Creative! Decorative! Happy filled! Occasional pleasure! Healthy missing!

These are all the cutest things that a party must hold but... beyond these there are some secret happenings that we as an individual can feel. The excitement! Before a happy festive or a party, the future focused thoughts would make me delight. This excitement will add a cherry to my mood which is spreadable. Lots and lots of small things can make us happy and make us to fall in love with. If we start to cheer those things, then we are the happiest person.

Everybody loves to love. Yes, I am in the topic. Romance!

We all love someone. Some might express and some might be confidential. The curiosity lies in the confidential love but the responsibility lies in holding the expressed love. Everything is simple but it lies in how we handle and taking it. Before loving someone make sure that you could handle them at any situation without leaving their hands. Love is not just having crush or some excited feeling on others but it has more and more beyond that.

It is full of UNDERSTANDING!

Understanding is not that much tough to follow. It is just predicting, what would be the next move of your partner. You can wonder! But that is true and the truest!

How to forecast? Is there any formula?

Yes! Of course we have! Before entering into a relationship just know about your partner. What he/she likes to do and foremost, what he/she don't likes. Try to analyse them first before entering into the relationship. But once it is done, just stick yourself with it. Everything in the world has ups and downs with which we are allowed to live with. Enjoy the positives and accept the negatives. This is the basic formula for a healthy relationship. Try to create n number of memories. Memories have the power of curing the unwanted scars of relationship.

Every day is not the same. Every moment won't give only happiness. There might be n number of sad shades but even you should sustain. That is the unregistered notice. But... one day you will be rewarded. It might take some days or months or years but sure you are going to lead an organised life. Nobody in this world is bad or unfit for relationship. It is all about the sense of understanding and forecasting. Everybody believes that some external power creates relationships and we are acting according to it. That's literally no. It is all about how we are getting attracted over one's traits and proceeding.

BREAK-UP?

This is the common word that every individual says when they get fed up with their loved one. Listen charms! Break up is something that means 'Breaking up the saddest portion and moving a level up in the relationship!'. Do I make sense? There is no one in the world who can care you like a true soul mate does. They will always move forward only to make you happy. They will hurt themselves only to prove their love. They will fight with you only to hold your hands till their last breathe. If they don't love you they won't fight. Only a true soul mate would even take you to the hardest situation to mould you.

So my dear charms! If you want your life to be colourful just enjoy the cutest fight hereafter! They care..! They fight...! They love...! Just give your limitless love and take back the infinite flawless results of it!

LOVE YOU...!

You! The Best person! The soul mate! □
I feel blessed to be under your shade of love. I know all the flaws that had happened between us are a moulding process for our future. I accept and I never regret! Thank you for making me special in your life like nobody does. I've grown a lot mentally to make our future and I am ready to face any obstacles with you. You can even get me to the hell but just hold my hands. I am ready to support you till my last muscle gets decayed.

You are my mentor!
You are my support!
You are my Hero!
You are my Villain!
You are my everything!

ETERNAL LOVE...!

Give more and take lot more! Loving is the best hobby that helps you to ignore negativity. It can keep your heart fresh and even it makes you to live long. I hope I gave very good life stuff because I have an endless love on my charms! Love everyone and hate no one! It'll surely do a magical change in your life. Before winding up my thought sharing, I wish you charms to have a great and colourful future ahead.

Let the love season begin and never ends!!

SWETHA PICHAIPILLAI

Swetha is an engineering graduate who is an Software engineer now. She has passion for art and writing and explores both the worlds with her imagination. She enjoys writing as much as she loves to paint. She is a very creative person who challenges her potential by try new things.

Instagram ID: swetha_pillai_

RIGHT NEXT TO ME

He was there standing right next to me, holding my hand as I was crying loudly because of the pain. It was the first time I fell down and scratched the whole of my left hand. He walked me home, stayed right next to me till my mind had calmed down, I tried to sleep and the pain was fading away. I felt soft hands stroking my little fangs, after a little while it stopped.

As I was falling asleep, I heard his mumbling voice saying, "I will be right next to her in the morning when she opens her eyes". There was a smile in my face as my consciousness faded into my own Dream land. I created my little Dream land after watching all those advertisements on TV.

My Dream land would have a little house with many shelves of candies and a big playground plus a huge garden. I dream about it all the time. It was on that day I started dreaming of having another person along with me. I invited him to my dreamland and shared my candies with him.

That day I wanted to wake up from my dream, I wanted to know if he was here. I slowly opened my right eye followed by the left to see him looking at me and he said "Hey Tara. Did you dream about Dream land? Was I there too?" with the softest smile. I became so happy because he was there, right next to me.

He was there! Arjun was there!

Arjun was my neighbor and we are in the same class in school. We stayed together all the time. Both our fathers work in the same office and by that our mothers too became friends and so did we, me and Arjun. Every day the first thing he asks me was if he was invited into my Dreamland.

I would tease him and say you will never get in it. When he asked me today, I just smiled and said "You sneaked in but I kicked you out". He made a little victory dance with his hands up in the air and said "Yes! So, I made it to the entrance. Not many days are left till I get my own little chair in your house." Controlling my laugh I said "In your dreams may be but definitely not mine".

We started laughing and in that moment the way I looked at him was starting to change without me even knowing it is. As time flew by, I was having these strange feelings but one thing was very clear to me 'I like him. I really like him a lot and felt heavenly while spending time with him. What about him?'. This made my heart pause every time I felt those unusual things inside me.

We entered High school before realizing it. We shared everything, we went through tough times together, we struggled in our exams together and passed it together too. One day as we were watching the sunset sitting on the swings of the park, I heard a dog crying for a second. I asked "Did you hear that?". "Hear what?", he asked with an unchanged face. Then. there was the sound again, I stopped and looked at him. He got off the swing and said "I think I heard some dog crying nearby".

"I was asking the same thing just now, you idiot", I yelled. "Well, you did not mention a dog is crying somewhere", he said.

"She may be hurt", I said. "Yeah, maybe. But why would it be 'She'?", he asked me air coating the word 'her'. "I don't know, I just said it because I am a girl", I said.

"Very thoughtful of you. Crying puppy will be a girl", he said. We were about to fight but we heard the puppy cry again. We stopped and I said "Let's quickly look for the puppy and take her home". As he started looking with me, he said "Home you say. Interesting. Suppose if the puppy is a girl you can take her to your home and I will come there to play with her. If not then I will keep him and he will stay with me, you can visit if you want". I gave him an intense look and said "Deal. It will be a girl and you have to be coming to my home all the time hereafter", I chuckled. I really liked the idea of us staying together for a longer time because of the puppy and I wanted him next to me exactly like the time when I fell down.

"I am seeing an overconfident girl next to me. Just a heads up don't cry if the puppy is a boy, okay". He marched forward without waiting for a response. I was about to jump over him but I saw him crossing his right-hand fingers. Is he wishing for the puppy to be a boy? How selfish. I got so angry but just then I thought what if he is not. I stopped walking and watched him go behind the tree and a few minutes later he came back with a little biscuit color little puppy in his hand. He came near me and handed over the puppy. "So, what are you going to name her?", he said.

He said 'her'. It is a... Girl! The puppy is mine. I was so happy, I tried covering her body with my hand, it wasn't enough to cover her. I suddenly felt warmth covering my fingertips because of his hand. I turned to look at him and he was smiling. He doesn't look sad or angry but instead he looks kind of happy, so is he okay with me having the puppy, then did he wish for the puppy to be girl. For me? Did he? I really wanted to hear a loud voice shouting at me 'He did'. Since he did not get to have her, I asked him to name her. He rushed to me after a week and said "Let's name her 'Scooby'". "And that took you one week?", I teased him.

"Don't you know I love Scooby Doo and was I there in the Dream land today?", he asked to hear a 'Yes' for both of his questions. I smiled and said "Yes, I know you love it and no, you were executed for trespassing". He seemed a little upset hearing that which has been happening quite a while, before he used to say I will make it one day. I was wondering why. "Don't be so obsessed about it", I said but he did not say anything back. Still, we did end up naming her Scooby.

We started spending more time together because of Scooby. The days were becoming even more precious to me. I really have to thank Scooby for calling out. But that felt selfish, the poor girl was crying out in the cold. That day I dreamt about Scooby running around in my Dream land and we were laughing and chasing her together.

The next morning, I realized that I have been dreaming about him a lot lately and I haven't told him yet. I'm thinking about him a lot. I want him to be right next to me always. I know I like him. He does too, I have come to know that much in these years. But this strange feeling towards him I get now is I think may be... I... Love... Him... I love him. Oh my god, I love him. I started jumping on my bed.

Wait, What about him? Does he love me? These questions make my head spin but I have to push all these aside and try concentrating on my final exams. But, how can I? Even though I'm scared to tell I love him. I still want to. Because more than anything I wanted to know the answer to my question. To get it out, I took a small paper and wrote 'Arjun, you made it to my Dream land.' This is enough for now a paper can't handle it everything I want to tell him. I folded the paper and inserted it in a capsule and hanged it in Scooby's collar. I knew my secret would be safe with Scooby.

It was the last day of the exam, tomorrow morning I will talk to Arjun. After the exam ended, he came up to me and said "I need to tell you something." I was confused and said "Okay, let's go to the playground and talk". We sat there silently for half an hour. I thought maybe I should talk about what I wanted but that is tomorrow and wiped those thoughts out. With being irritated by the silence and him not saying one word, I asked him "What shall we do this summer?".

"We won't be able to do anything", was his reply with a little frustration not looking at me. "Why do you say that? Are you going somewhere?" I asked. He said "Yes".

"Sorry Tara, I don't want to leave you alone for the whole summer but my grandmother is sick. So, me and mom will be spending summer there taking care of Grandma", he looked sad. Really sad. As if he was going to cry but instead, I did. "So, you will be leaving me?", without being able to hold my tears I started crying. He stood up and said "I'm sorry for making you cry. I will see you by the end of summer. Bye, Tara" and he left. He did not wait to hear about what I wanted to tell him tomorrow. I went home. Scooby was by my side all along.

Every day we went to the playground and I waited for him. Scooby looks around for him for a while and comes back to me with a stick. That became her hobby now. Every night I touch the capsule and think "One day" and then fall asleep.

Summer would end next week, I never thought I would survive this long without seeing him. But somehow, I did. That next day I woke up and called Scooby because it was time for her to eat. She was nowhere in the house. I started looking for her thinking she would have gone to find a new stick. I started going to the place she usually goes and finally ended up in the playground. She was there playing with her new stick. When I called her, she came to me with it. I took it and was giving her scratches when I noticed the capsule in her collar was missing. "Scooby where did you drop the capsule. It was there yesterday night. What happened to it Scooby?" I asked and started crying. The only thing I was holding on to give to Arjun has gone missing. It may not be something big but it meant more at least for me.

"Are you looking for something?", I heard a voice.

After wiping my tears, I turned around and said "No, just..." my words stopped. I could not believe my eyes. He was there standing next to the swing and holding the capsule in his hand with his softest smile. I didn't blink, didn't move. I stood there like a statue as he walked towards. He smiled. I broke my stillness and smiled back. Maybe he would have taken Scooby for a walk

because I woke up late and she would have been jumping on him excitedly seeing him after a long time and because of that the capsule would have fallen and he might have taken it. Wait, the capsule. Did he open it and see what was inside it? Before I could think it through and wonder if he read what I wrote in it, he broke my silence and asked me, "So I made it to the Dream land, huh?" I couldn't believe he is here and he read it. He read the paper read what I wrote for him. I happily said, "Yes, you made it" with tears in my eyes and smiled. He came closer and wiped my tears and held my cheek and he said "I was sad I would never make it." and then his head touched mine.

"Why were you so worried about coming into my Dream land?", I asked him.

"You don't remember? When you first told me about your dream land for the first time, you said you have included all the things you love. After my feelings towards you started to change, I thought when you love me, I will be in it too. That was the reason why I became obsessed with knowing the answer for that every day", he said scratching his head.

I wasn't expecting to hear something like that. All this time he did… he did love me back. I was so stupid to realize it this late. If I had known the hidden meaning in his question, I would have told the truth a long time back. Silly me, I just always teased him when he asked me. I smiled and said, "You were not wrong. I do."

"You do what?", he asked with a confused expression.

"I… Love you. I love you Arjun. I do", I said in a voice he could barely hear and slowly looked at him. His eyes were wide open in shock and then with a smile he said "I… Love you too Tara. I promise I will always stay right next to you".

"I know."

NAMRATHA ATLURI

Namratha Atluri is a persuing MBA graduate, a blogger acted as a Host and Chief Co-ordinator for several events like Fenestra, Entreprenuer development programme, workshops on Microsoft Office, Statistical Package For Social Sciences, Cyberlaws on Women, Women Empowerment and Technical Estrades. Qualified for Associate Company Secretary Foundation.

Instagram ID: _justtlikethiss____

LOVE FOR LANGUAGE BECAUSE LANGUAGE MATTERS!

Many people who speak more than one language switch personalities when they switch languages. In this era of Globalization, everyone is able to connect with each other on the basis of language. In fact language is a medium through which your able to read this book . Language is in every aspect of our lives. Can we imagine ourselves communicating with each other without a language.., hard isn't it?

Acquiring a language is not only learning grammar or vocabulary; it is learning new sounds, expressions and our change in perceptions. Why do we need to learn a new language…?

Thinking on several aspects on what benefits us from learning a new language.., it enables us in making better decisions, improves memory, increase attention span, better cognitive abilities, improved first language and of course a bigger brain. Knowing a foreign language other than the native language has been proven to be extremely beneficial, be it in Financial or Social aspect ! It is observed that in parts of Europe students learning a foreign language is 100%, across the whole Europe the median is 92%.. India has got into the race showing its highest demand for languages like French, German, Spanish, Mandarin and Japanese.

In Today's world In the race of today's generation a foreign language is essential in develop as well as sustain a strong footing in the global economy It not only helps in making new contacts but also in gaining job opportunities and building good career by improving self-worth. Business enlargement globally is possible only by acquiring foreign languages. People associated with social services need to work with diverse groups from several countries and the ability to speak in foreign language enables them to serve much better. The next important decision to be made is to decide which foreign language to learn, whether you learn a language out of your interest or a specific reason it is a long term process and success, it opens up several doors of opportunities in front of you. I see the learning new languages as an ocean the deeper it goes the livelier it becomes. The more languages you acquire the better you can express yourself!

Learning language with technology: To learn a language is to have one more window from which to look at the world. Technology is very much similar to a question of learning by doing. An inspiring aspect of this technology is its ability to reach the audience worldwide. In the context of learning language through technology it connects teachers from one corner of the world with their student in the other corner of the world. Technology has been an important part of teaching and learning environment. According to Pourhosein Gilakjani (2013), by using the technology great changes can be brought to existing language teaching methods. Pourhosein Gilakjani and Sabouri (2014) emphasized that by using technology learners can have a control on their own learning process and may get access to many information over which their teacher may not control. How far is technology efficient in learning new language…?

- Technology can be used as teaching tool, teaching resource, learning tool and learning resource.

- Technology offers a dozens of tools in real time to help learners. Students are enabled to access
- Dictionaries
- Browse internet in the language they are learning
- Find pen pals, conversation partners
- Find online tutors
- Facebook, Linkedin, Instagram and Twitter offer a daily a smorgasboard of language learning practice.

Technology can make language learning more effective by enabling learners to record themselves by the language they are learning outside the class and bring the recordings into the class room for review and feedback.Through chatting learners can communicate during the classes it is beneficial for the learning process because it allows learners time to reflect and review their output. The learners feel much more motivated in doing online courses and online skill development due to their other commitments in their daily life. By using devices they even feel it beneficial as they can attend a session by carrying it out to different places. Grammar checkers can also be implemented in three different ways i.e syntax based checker, statistics based checker and rule based checker. In these the texts are completely parsed, sentences are completely analyzed and assigned with a tree structure.

A language model which contains a large training corpus including many short phrases that can be used for detecting and correcting grammar errors. Best applications for learning languages 2020

- Babble gives the best online school experience in acquiring new language and for further guidance in the new language.
- Mondly is a application which helps in remembering specific phrases
- Duolingo is the best application for learning multiple languages.
- Memrise is suitable for learning to speak casually in a new language.
- Busuu is best for goal oriented users
- Lirica is a wonderful application for learning Spanish musically.
- Drops is best for the visual learners
- Language learning with Netflix is best for breaking down how a language works.
- Pimsleur is the application for learning on the go
- Rosetta Stone ia best for auditory learners.

Looking at ocean of opportunities we are left with, it just takes a click to reach what we want .You can never understand one language until you understand atleast two…! I say we are privileged, hope you too. Building up career with foreign languages   You have to learn the rules of the game and then you have to play better than anyone else. What's this foreign language worth…? Remember you can't have the fruits without the roots… Ever wondered on what fruits we can receive on sowing this skill…! This information will give you an idea on the various career opportunities we are left with after acquiring a foreign language.

Career opportunities

Teacher, Private tutor or Online tutor in this anyone who knows a foreign language can get a job as a classroom teacher and in has a good scope in Schools, colleges, Universities. They are and less availability. Private teachers where they work on one-on-one and face-to-face basis. As there is an option for working freelance in the job they can have complete control on the methods they can use and on the lessons.

There are sites such as Craigslist, Monster, eBay Classifieds or Oodle were their services can be posted.

- One of the smart way to reach out for tutoring clients is by signing up for Wyzant.

- Online tutor blows out the opportunity to enhance oneself in a wider market. This idea of working whenever and wherever appeals to oneself and they cannot be limited by time or geography anymore.

- Verbling is hands-down the best for online tutoring jobs.

- FluentU account can provide with relevant video materials and inspiration for your lessons and also in staying up-to-date on cultural trends and references.

Interpreter is probably doing some kind of "bridging". Where you're facilitating communication between parties in a situation, similar to when two heads of a state who don't know each other's language need to talk to each other. Interpreters are commonly visible in public events like MISS UNIVERSE PAGEANT, UFC, Church where majority of the crowd may not understand what the speaker is trying to convey but are interested in knowing what it can be. Learning a new language becomes a surviving pill.

Translator, If this working next to MISS UNIVERSE isn't your cup of tea then probably working with the written form of language is yours. Translator work behind the scenes unlike interpreters who take their place in the spotlight Translators take up a crucial role in our society and are of different types such as Literary translators and Specialized translators who work for different fields. Legal Translator, within the field of law such as protocols, decrees, decisions, depositions, even minutes of proceedings and contracts. Medical Translator, can make physicians, diagnosis, treatment plans, patient information and instructions intelligible in a different language. We have good book for translating.

Children's Book Writer, it is a good way to start writing, children's literature has various aspects of humanity. In addition to racial, gender and cultural issues it has effectively tackle certain social arrangements. Learning foreign language isn't just the knowing a different set of sounds in the same concept. A different language is essentially another view of the world.

Blogger, Seller and Speaker when you are good in a foreign language you can express your vision on a greater volume and a better way. It increases your marketing and enhances your potential. But most important part is that the blog must meet a specific language need or it must having a particular angle, rather that just being a general repository of the rants. Speaker and seller part really comes after a considerable following for the blog.

You Tuber or Podcaster, with the technology with have around us we can create our own channel in minutes in case of you tube where the teacher can upload teaching videos. Unlike video lessons, podcasts allow listeners to multitask so you can deliver your lessons while the listeners can do other work.

We have YouTube ideas and Podcasting insights to get you started.

Tour Guide, Learning a foreign language gives an opportunity in becoming a tourist guide in a foreign land, we also see that many tourists would choose international tour packages arranged by their own countrymen instead of those from the target country.

Liaison Officer, A liaison officers are the face and the force of the parties they normally represent. Liaison acts as a glue that holds up two distinct parties as one. Liaison is a job beyond a job of a interpreter or a translator because liaising requires a much more active role. Anyone with great skills in co-ordination and communication can give this role a try.

Researcher (Field), most of the human knowledge especially from the past is not recorded in English. There aren't much people working on certain ancient texts. In case you are interested in on unveiling knowledge of the past then an foreign language is good to use there. Market research and Environmental research can also be related with today's world.

Skill up yourself with foreign languages from Inlinguachennai.com The career decisions you are making today will affect the opportunities you have tomorrow.

SANTHOSH PANDIAN A

SANTHOSH PANDIAN A is from Chennai. He is one who loves to do more volunteering work. He is passionate about helping people who needs help to survive or for Education.
Instagram ID: santhosh__pandian

AMOR DE LA VIDA
PARENTS LOVE

Love is a beautiful feeling in this world. The world functions because of love. Every human being get into the earth by love. Yes, you are a gift of your parents love. First love for all of us is our parents. It is the purest form of love. They care for us their entire life. That love is pure because it does not expect anything back from us. Their love is always different from others. Even if we break them, their love towards us never changes. A child gets three stages of love from their parents. First one at a younger age, by caring you keeping you healthy and teaching you basics of life with their love. Second, feeding you the knowledge to survive and show good vibes to society. Third, parents finding a love for you. Wow, what a beauty! Bringing you by love to get into love.

MOTHER AND SISTER LOVE

"Mother" the purest word in the world. Not an only word, but it's also a belief, a pure belief to every child in this world. We all get scolding's from our mother after that when you are down, the first person to console you is our mother. Her love for her children is like an ocean that goes deep without any end. If you want to achieve anything in your career, she will support you with her love and affection. When you achieve anything small, she celebrates it as a big achievement.

My younger sister is my second mother. Her concern and love towards me is unbelievable. Since she is younger than me, her caring is unmatchable. Whenever my mom is not there, she takes care of my sickness. I am quite poor in English. She always helped to improve that. She helps to do a lot of assignments.

FRIENDS LOVE

Love from friends always has a special and strong place in my heart. It never disappears nor is forgotten by friends. We meet many people in our life with whom we share a lot of feelings and respect for us. But some are odd ones from everyone.

When a good group of friends is together with a positive attitude, there will be a success. There will be a fight with a group of friends, but none of us leave the other. I am going to share my personal experience with my friends. I struggled to pay college fees that lead to discontinuing my studies.

I told my friends everything they contributed their money to part of my fee and supported me to continue my studies. Some friends support me with their positive energy. These things made me work hard in my career. That is friend's love. It will stay with me till my last breath.

Not only financial help but also a lot of little sacrifices they made to make me happy. I always prefer to go to a friend's home instead of relatives. I feel comfortable over there.

A friend is one who comes along with you in difficult times in life. Sometimes he finds the solution; sometimes, he consoles you. But they are always there and you have a shoulder to lean on. The first person we meet after our parents is friends, it starts there and continues throughout our life. All the strangers we meet in a certain stage of our life may become friends and, it is the beauty of friendship. As Former President, Dr. A.P.J. Abdul Kalam said, "One best book is equal to hundred good friends but, one good friend is equal to a library." As legend said, one good friend, grooms your character and attitude.

FIRST LOVE

Our first love towards a person is unconditional. I love the way you care about me. What type of relationship it may be, Trust plays a major role? I have never broken your trust. We had a good understanding. The memories we created and the hard times that we handled together will be cherished till my breath. The days we hang out, the days we sit and chat about our future, was blissful. But all this happiness had become a daydream. You left me with nothing and took all my happiness and smile. You left me halfway and, all my dreams and memories that I planned to build with you were drowned. The days become dark, and the nights become hell. I knew how it would be for you but, it was hard for me to accept the truth. I hope that you have the good life that you wished to have without me. Have a happy life and stay blessed.

CRICKET LOVE

Cricket is a game where all of us United celebrate together. We can see it everywhere. Love for cricket apart from the ages, from child to grandparents. When I was 12, I got attached to cricket. I started watching cricket in Word Cup 2011, we won with an enormous team effect, that is my first cricket experience and, I fell in love with that. After that, I followed cricket very closely to know the proper rules and regulations. And also, I started to watch some old classic matches to relive the moments, that much cricket has attracted me. My special format of cricket is the test. I love test cricket. It actually connected with our life. We go through difficult phases in life. Maybe financially, you are not that well off, or maybe the mortgage has suddenly gone up, but you ride the difficult times in search of the better times thereafter. You never give up in difficult times. Test cricket is exactly like that.

PROFESSION LOVE

Profession is mandatory for everyone. In this world, everyone has something to do, whether they are interested or not but they are involved in some profession. Love for profession should always be there to succeed in your life. You need to work hard and smart in your profession, which improves your reputation in that society. Profession is hard to succeed sometimes it leads to sacrifice your own family, happiness, etc. The medical profession is the most respected in the world. No matter where you work, you as a doctor, lead a life of dignity and respect. Many of my friends, had a desire to do Doctor, but few took it seriously to achieve it. Their mind and thoughts about their profession are clear. They started to sacrifice their happiness with family sometimes, they, get away from home to join in college. These things made them strong to achieve in their profession.

SOCIAL SERVICE LOVE

The most important love for everyone in their life. Humanity is one of the rare things in this world. What should be social service? Nothing. When your walking on the road, old age people trying to cross the road, help them. You spend your quality time for them. The happiest people I know are those who lose themselves in the service of others. - Gordon B. Hinckley If you do that, your entire day will be happy, it is a small help but it has an impact on your life. It is not our job, but even when you do that it shows your humanity. I love to go to old age homes and help, that really gave me more happiness than anything. They are broken, but whenever you meet them, they happily talk to you as like your grandparents. My love for this is never gonna end. Do service, show humanity to the world.

SAJIN JENIFER.A.S

Sajin Jenifer.A.S. is from Chennai, through the passion of flying her dream was always to become a pilot and she studied aeronautical engineering. She is currently doing her MBA from St. Josephs college of engineering. She loves reading novels and her favourite author is Chetan Bhagat. UNKNOWN CHANGES OF LIFE is her first anthology and she is interested in writing more anthologies. She is an extrovert and hyperactive. She likes to travel a lot and loves to create memories. She is planning to start her own business after a few years. She always is an ever smiling girl and always cool.

Instagram ID: sajin_jenifer

UNKNOWN CHANGES OF LIFE
CHAPTER 1

It was a hectic day shopping all day for travelling to Kerala. The travel which I did not expect to change my life completely. So, this is going to be a short story of my love of my life. Myself Samarah born and living in Chennai. Basically, I am a girl who loves reading novels and always I love fantasy. I am an open-minded girl who always likes to talk a lot. In, India it is always a mandatory rule of parents to marry their kids at the age of 23 or 24 older than that a girl goes it is seen as she has become so old. So, it happened to me unknown changes of my life. My dad told me that we have to visit our grandmother for new year after all the packaging my mom and I started to travel towards the airport. The flight was a midnight flight always a midnight flight was an irritating one. It was 29th December 2019 midnight 2 am the flight has to be departed at 3.30 am. We were waiting at airport for the flight it was indigo. After waiting for the flight and munching my favourite lays. And we go into the flight and after a one-hour flight travel we reach Trivandrum airport. From there we move to our home. It was a great shock there my dad was planning to make me meet a guy. It was a great shock as it was the first time. I am going to meet a guy and his parents for a marriage proposal I did not have the time to put on my favourite makeup but had time to just apply kajal and tie a ponytail. Then in a white car he arrived in the first meet I did not think he would be my future. There I saw him the guy with broad muscular shoulders fair tall as 6 feet wearing a dark blue shirt and grey pant. He looked kind of handsome maybe. Then slowly he walked into the house and sat. Marriages in India are kind a weird, people have to sit and watch the girls as if the girls are showroom dolls and they chose whom they like. It was kind a weird feeling taking cups of coffee and going and standing next to a guy, that was the first time I saw Samrath so closely and after I offered the coffee to him, I sat opposite to him. From the corner of his eyes, he was looking top to bottom how I look and finally he paused for a few seconds to look at my face. After a few minutes of silence, we were allowed to talk personally. We walked outside the house and sat at the chairs placed outside the house then I noticed that he was wearing the same colour dress which I was wearing so immediately I told to Samrath same pinch and he looked at his shirt and me and gave a small smile and we were talking casually and he did not give any eye contact to me but was talking looking at the plants around the house. Then deep inside my mind came a feeling that he doesn't like me. While we were still talking, he immediately stopped me talking and said shall we go in and I got little disturbed and we moved in.

CHAPTER 2

After a few minutes of happy talks Samrath and his parents walked outside the house. Samrath looked at me and gave a small smile and immediately after they went it will be the obvious question that many parents ask did you like the guy? Immediately, without a doubt I said no I did not like the guy. My parents did not force me into the marriage, then I happily ran into the room and took my phone and made a call to my sisters and told what happened and told that I did not like Samrath and days passed and it was new year we were happy to enter 2020.

Days kept passing on and then I was as usual going back to my college and having fun with my friends I was doing master's in business administration every time I think about this course, I always remember that I just joined this course to extend my marriage time. So, I chose to do this course to just to try to gain more time for marriage. I was studying my MBA in one of the strictest colleges in Chennai, but even though the college was strict I was having a fun time with my friends and even to my friends I talked about Samrath how he was and how he behaved and told to them that I did not like him and will not accept him.

After reaching back from college to my home, my mom gave another shock that Samrath's parents are coming to see me this weekend, then I started arguing with my mom that I did not like the guy how will you make his parents come to see me and I am not going to marry that guy. Then my mom was convincing me that they are just coming to see you and we will do as you wish if you don't like the guy, we won't marry you to him. Then, I had a little bit relief and I went to my room to take a nap. In my dream came his face, the same fair and tall muscular Samrath we both are talking to each other.

Then, I woke from my sleep and took my phone and contacted my friend and talked about my dream and about his parents coming to visit me this weekend. My friend immediately told there must be something between you both God is matchmaking for you both. Immediately, I got irritated and cut the call. Then, I was thinking what my friend told why is this guy again and again coming in my life. I was so much confused he did not show his face and talk to me I hoped that he would have gone and told his parents that he hates me. Are his parents forcing him into this marriage, within a minute my mind gives me million thoughts then I realise why on earth am I thinking so much about a guy whom I hate a lot? Then I ran down the steps and took a cup of coffee and all of a sudden, I felt more refreshed.

CHAPTER 3

It was the weekend the day his parents were coming to meet me again but this time there was a difference Samrath was not present to see me. My whole house was busy cleaning all the floors, arranging the sofas, arranging the tables, placing all the snacks in the plates and the plates was loaded with delicious egg puffs steaming hot and its smell was calling me to take a bite and all types of sweets in the plates ladoo,jalebi,kaju katli and so on. In the glasses fresh orange juice was poured and my mom was busy making tea and I was standing in the kitchen with my night gown and sleepy eyes within a second my dad came into the kitchen and told me to get ready fast they have reached near our home and I immediately ran and went into the bathroom and took a quick bath and came out and wore a long pink chudi with gold dupatta then I tie my hair with a good hairstyle and wore my favourite jhumkas and wore silver colour bangles and applied eyeliner and kajal in my eyes and applied a matching lipstick for`my lips and I looked in the mirror turning left and right and finally I was happy with my whole look.

Then, after a few minutes Samrath's parents arrived and as usual I was carrying a plate in which were cups of hot tea the only that was running in my mind was, I should not drop the tea on his parents then as I moved towards the hall, I noticed there were two extra women at the age of mid-forties sitting next to them they both were wearing saree and they both was looking at me from top to bottom and scanning me. They gave a warm smile to me and I smiled back I placed the tea in the table and each one took their cup and as each one was drinking their tea and they were asking questions like what are you studying? where are you studying? What are your future plans? I was answering to all questions they were asking me and after they drank their tea, and they were asking about Samrath and I did not show much interest to them and then they were brainwashing me telling me good about him and you will be happy with him. Then, Samrath's mom started talking to me that my son doesn't like to come to Chennai then I said that I like to stay in Chennai taking a separate house. Then his mother was asking questions like, do you wear saree and my dad said yes, she knows to wear saree and I looked at my dad giving a weird reaction that when on earth did, I tie a saree and his mother was again asking me do you know to cook and I said no before my dad is going to interrupt me. Then his mother told that after your both marriage you will move to Bangalore with him. Immediately I stopped her and told that I was not interested to move from Chennai to any other place. Then a small argument started between his mom and me.

CHAPTER 4

It was very weird that his mother and I was arguing with the issue and I said that I am not interested to marry your son. Then his father was trying to convince me to marry his son and I was still in the mood of not accepting him. After an hour they finished their talking and they were planning to leave they was walking down the steps while they were reaching the gate his mom and dad came back and started speaking to me and they were telling that his son was a very good guy and will take good care of me and in my mind it was running that all parents will say the same thing about their sons quiet obvious and they was trying to brainwash me again telling that Samrath and you are going to stay alone in Bangalore no one is going to disturb you after a few years you can return back to Kerala. While this conversation was going by a side one of the aunties told that Samrath was a very good guy and please don't lose a good guy in life. Then, his dad told I will bring my son again you both talk together and decide we all really like you both together. Then they left, then me as usual started yelling at Samrath in my mind. Then that night they called and told that my dad that Samrath will be visiting me this week and all of a sudden, I had an excitement as well as an irritation. Then my mind tells me a word ok you just wait and see what is going to happen. Then as usual days passed by and my boring life kept on moving. Then on Friday my dad received a call from Samrath's dad saying that they won't be visiting us this weekend because Samrath is having a work and they will be visiting us after two weeks and I was feeling a bit relived and my days passed by exams and projects and again we received

a call that they will visit after a week because the work is not finished yet and deep in my mind I was thinking that maybe he hates me and so he is not visiting and then I realize that even I don't like him then why must I think about him and I started doing my work. Then our lent season began as Christians we don't do any functions during this lent period and so my meeting with Samrath was postponed to a month and the most unexpected things happened in everyone's life the arrival of the most dangerous known virus in history the COVID-19 or corona virus. Due to this virus all the schools and colleges was shut down and within a week everything was shut down the factories, shops, malls everything even groceries shop was available for a few hours. It was not just in India but it was throughout the world, the count of the people affected by the virus kept on increasing day by day and the death rate was also increasing immensely. Everyone would have had the fear of corona even I had it. Since the cases keep on increasing in Chennai we planned to move to stay in Kerala for 3 to 4 months. We reached Kerala and we were peacefully staying and even in Kerala the cases kept on increasing. Then we received a call suddenly after 2 months stay in Kerala from Samrath's father.

CHAPTER 5

In the phone call Samrath's father told that can we come and meet Samarah this weekend and immediately my dad told yes and after he disconnected the call, I started arguing with my parents that I am not going to meet him and said that they were first telling they were coming to see me in Chennai and now they are telling they are coming to meet me here, they like me and if the guy likes me tell him to come to Chennai. My dad agreed to what I said and called his dad and told him that we are going back to Chennai this week can you come and visit us after that and even his parents agreed to the idea. In my mind I was thinking that I am going to say no whatever happens also. Then we moved back to Chennai that week it was September the COVID-19 after 6 months from march was little bit reduced. Then it was the day I was again going to meet him September 27th the day I thought I will reject him.

As Samrath was going to come to visit me we went to buy new clothes I bought a silk maroon colour chudhidar with gold border in the bottom of my chudi top. The dress looked too traditional and I liked it. In the night I told my mom why is it you don't see me any other guy. Then my mom said that it was not us who are arranging this meeting we also told that you did not like him but the guy said that he liked you so only his parents called and arranged to meet you again. I got a shock all of a sudden and thought what did Samrath like me so many months I thought he hated me so I hated him even more suddenly a point of excitement began in me I was thinking about Samrath. It was 27th of September as usual my house busy cleaning since they are going to come and I was little excited and it a little bit irritated really I did like Samrath. Everyone was excited in my house my mom and dad, my two elder sisters everyone. Immediately after a few minutes they arrived and I went into the room and my sister came running and told me that the guy looks so beautiful and my sister's mother-in-law told that don't miss this guy he is totally matching for you and all of a sudden, I was double minded should I accept or not. I carried cups of tea and went to the second floor to meet him and his parents there I saw him with white shirt and little green pant and a brown belt he was more handsome than the first time I saw him and I gave tea to everyone and after everyone drank tea, they made us talk personally. We walked downstairs and we started talking there was so much smile in Samrath's face that I did not expect this reaction from him and he was so excited to see me and he immediately started talking to me and he asked, how are you? After a very long gap we are meeting and I replied ya I am good and yes, it's been 9 months seeing you. Then he was smiling at me and I asked him do you like me and he replied yes, I liked you a lot and it gave me slight shock then again, I asked him do you really like me?

CHAPTER 6

After hearing the same question again Samrath started to laugh and replied yes, I liked you so only I waited so long and came again to see, hearing this from him immediately gave butterflies in my stomach and I started blushing and we kept on talking and he asked me do you like to travel? I replied yes, I love to travel and he told that he loves to travel and I told hereafter we will travel together and he smiled at me with his glittering eyes and I asked him will you take good care of me and he told that to take care of you only I am marrying you I will take care of you. After a few minutes of talking, we both were blushing seeing each other and I asked him shall I say ok for the marriage and he replied say fast for this only I was waiting for 9 months and we smiled at each other and we both walked together and I came near him and checked the height I looked so short next to him. We walked up the stairs and both of our parents was looking at us and my dad asked me seeing my happy face do you like the guy and I told yes my dad went into a deep shock that for 9 months I was cursing this guy and now I am blushing for him and my dad again called me and asked really did you like the guy or you are just saying simply so I would get upset and I answered no I really like the guy a lot and my dad was very happy seeing my reply and immediately my parents and his parents was talking about our engagement and marriage and his mom told his birthday is on October 7th and he is turning 26 this year and I noted the date in my mind to wish him and after all the discussions they ate lunch from my home and they left and Samrath and I was looking at each other and smiling and I thought he would ask my phone number but he did not ask it. He said bye and left the home. I immediately called my friends and told that I told ok for Samrath and everyone was excited and I shared the selfie which we both took together. Each one told that we both look great together and you are a made for each other couple. I was so happy that finally I and Samrath joined together. I thought the next day he would ask my dad for my contact number and contact me but he did not do it and I was waiting for him to call and after so much fed up I myself asked my dad to get his number and give and I was eagerly waiting to wish for his birthday at midnight itself. At October 6th I was pasturing my dad to get his number but it was already late and my dad told we will call in the morning and ask his number. So, I became very much upset and went and slept I was very angry on Samrath that he did not call me still. Then next day morning my dad got his number and gave but I was so angry on him that I did not take the number after a few minutes my hand automatically dialled his number and I called him. In two rings he picked up the call and before I wished him, he asked how did you know my birthday then I told him that I noted while your mom said and he laughed.

CHAPTER 7

After talking for a few minutes, he said that I am in work will call you back and after a few minutes he called back but I was in my online classes and so I could not take the call. At the evening, he himself called me and we were talking for hours and we did not even realise how the time was going so fast. Then we cut the call and after a few hours he called again and we were chatting about how we met and stuffs like what we like etc. The days was passing by he was in Kanyakumari and I was in Chennai truly it was the worst days of our life because we both were so deep in love but we can't see each other daily. Each day we were talking for hours in phone call as well as video call. Then there was a great idea to meet each other, there was a family function so I invited him, he was very happy to come but due to work he could not come. Samrath was a civil engineer his work was always hectic so this was our first fight I fought with him and did not talk with him for not coming to meet me and I blocked his contact. Then after some time I unblocked and immediately he told I am coming, then we were so happy to meet each other after a month. It was the function day and the day I was going to meet him we planned a lot of stuffs. He arrived at my home with his brother and when his brother went out, I sat next to him we both were looking at each other and immediately Samrath gave me a kiss on my cheek. The kiss gave me butterflies in my stomach and I kissed him back in his cheek and we went off to the function. My dad sent me with Samrath and his brother. I and Samrath got so excited and we went together we both were sitting next to each other on the backseat of the car and we were holding hands. We cannot control our feelings and we started kissing each other we did not even mind that his brother was driving the car. Samrath placed his hands on my hips and was holding it gently and he kissed in my lips a soft kiss for a second and he took his lips away. In the whole function we were talking and playing with each other we were enjoying a lot. We were thinking we are going to miss each other after the function gets over. When the function was about to get over Samrath's dad told to me that Samrath was not concentrating on his job he is fully talking to you from morning to night. I said no we talk only in the evenings. Then while my dad was speaking to his dad, he told the same thing to him and while we returned home my dad told me to reduce the time talking to Samrath. Samrath gave me many surprises on that day he bought a unicorn doll, a rose, a bag full of chocolates, a box of donuts and a diamond ring. Every day, he was calling me early in the morning and in the evenings. Day by day my love for Samrath kept on increasing we were deeply in love. Each day my morning alarm was his phone call.

CHAPTER 8

Our second meeting came and I was travelling to Kerala for a marriage and I was going to meet him. We both were very excited. He came to my house and he hugged me and kissed me on my lips this was a long kiss we bought felt each other's body touching he was rubbing my back and I was hugging him tightly we kept on kissing each other and our tongues was touching and after a few minutes we stopped kissing and look at each other's face and smiled this time also he bought me many gifts. Day by day we were getting closer and even our engagement date was nearing. After few days we had another big fight and I was not talking to him but it was the toughest task which I ever did and after a few hours I spoke with him again and he told me please don't fight with me I can't be without talking with you. Immediately, tears started to pour from my eyes. I told him I miss him very badly I want to see him and immediately he came to Chennai that weekend. We both were in high on love mood while he came to Chennai, we both kissed each other hugged each other and we can't control our feelings and immediately he started kissing me wildly after a few minutes of kisses he carried me and spun me around I was so happy I was like flying in the air. We both were playing talking and enjoying our day as usual while he was returning back to Kanyakumari, I was missing him badly. We were talking over the phone while he was travelling my life was feeling complete while I was next to him. I did not know time can move so fast. Every time we talk over the phone 3 to 4 hrs just flies. Every night I will think of him before going to sleep and imagine our romances and blush. Love is magic it can happen to anyone in life, it will change their life completely. I could not imagine a day without him. One of the best things which happened in my life was him all my loneliness he took away. He was not just a fiancée but he was my best friend I can share with him anything he was also the same he shares with me everything. He was a caring dad too always he cared for me and stood for me in all situations. You are my precious treasure like a treasure that only I can open. I just can't wait for the day when our marriage occurs. I can't wait for the day to sleep next to you in the night and wakeup next to you in the morning. I love you Samrath. Every time I fight with you, you are the one who comes and speaks with me. I don't know if I am worth for your love but I will love you till my last breath. Each one will have a love in life so did Samarah had one which long lasting and forever like the eternal love.

      To know more what happened in Samarah and Samrath life please follow my next anthologies yours loving author Sajin Jenifer.

Flairs and Glairs, a platform by a student for the students. We are esteemed youth struggling to carve out our path for our future and we follow a basic mindset Since everyone is not born with all-round skills. Joining hands with people who are born to execute it with perfection is the best way to evolve. Self-Evolution is the need of the hour but, evolving as a community is what we strive for. The initiative as kickstarted by, Founder- Mr. Shubham Shah with the motive to utilize the skillset and talent of writing has now a team of 10+ people who are actively participating into newer forms of learning and discovering talents among youngsters. We Provide platform and services like Publishing opportunities, Open mics, Workshops, Hands-on training. Operating with Brand Name of Flairs and Glairs (Publication House), we offer the chance of elevating a passionate writer to an esteemed author With Brand name Teekhe Zasbaaat. We bring to you an opportunity to get accustomed with the Public Speaking and Presenting of Thoughts along with regular challenges to brush up your inking spirit. The newest initiative to extend our services we introduced in a new writing Platform- The Glittering Fables and Ink Over Tears.

We Choose to Fly Like A Falcon than to be

a Leg Pulling Crab.

To Know More: Infoline – 7781900870
Mail Us At-
flairsandglairs@gmail.com / info@flairsandglairs.in
Or Visit is at
www.flairsandglairs.com / www.flairsandglairs.in
Social Handles- @flairsandglairs @teekhezasbaaat